T0365358

About the Book

The book is based on a true story within a privately owned forest preserved for the minds of creative people. Mossy trails with interesting twists and turns are lined with homemade fairy houses. After our family's loss of a child, we decided to gather a community of friends to use our land as a magical place to go for peace and to connect back to nature. We asked friends and family to write their own fairy characters, and some are used in the book.

The main character in the book has suffered the loss of a sibling. She is asked to watch the family cat for five days, which she is not very interested in doing. She has many complaints about this chore. She—being a doctor, mother, and wife (and not in a good frame of mind)—feels overwhelmed with life.

It starts to happen on the first day. While going to the house to check on the cat, she ventures into the woods only to discover a whole new dimension of life. While she is walking on the path looking for the cat, she trips over a tree root and falls. She is not sure if she has injured her head or if what she sees next is real. She meets a figment of her imagination named Rosy. While lying on the ground, the character sketches what she sees. Rosy is an old spirit who guides her each day through the woods.

The next morning, the fairy spirit is revealed in the sketchbook, which begins the character's true-to-life journey. Each day for five consecutive days, she returns to feed the cat and ventures back into the woods. She meets different fairies, and she has extraordinary experiences. Once she enters through the gate, she is transported physically to the fairy realm. She gets introduced to many of the fairy characters and is impressed with their diversity as they show their own personalities and special gifts. On the last day, through the evidence of her drawings, she becomes aware that this is not just her mind playing tricks on her. For her, it is a personal journey—discovering how to enjoy the simple things in life just as she did when she was a child. She is shown that her sibling is still with her and lives on in the afterlife, filling the emptiness in her heart.

The photography in the book will make readers feel like they are taking the adventure with her. We know that nature has its own way of healing the human spirit in ways beyond our comprehension. This story is a light read and can only make us feel that love is all around, even when we feel alone.

The real character and illustrator goes through the grieving process and slowly begins to heal using her creative mind. She went back to college and received awards for her drawings. It has enlightened and changed her life. We hope that the readers will find their own personal creative self while taking a walk through these pages.

The Fairy Forest

BARBARA COSTANZA

Illustrated by
Melissa Sallah

Photography by
Susann Gude

Copyright © 2016 by Barbara Costanza. 726174
Library of Congress Control Number: 2016900341

ISBN: Softcover   978-1-5144-4955-4
        Hardcover   978-1-5144-4956-1
        EBook   978-1-5144-4954-7

Print information available on the last page

Rev. date: 04/11/2016

To order additional copies of this book, contact:
Xlibris
1-888-795-4274
www.Xlibris.com
Orders@Xlibris.com

ACKNOWLEDGMENT

I would like to thank the friends that kindly shared their creative fairy stories:

Debra Napoli, Marianne Patti, Maryanne Turvin,

Susan Meyer-Corbett, Gail Mauck, and Sheila Kilvington.

Their stories helped to mend our broken hearts and inspired the storybook to grow.

All their fairy spirits are still living in the woods, preserved just for them.
A special thanks to Keri Sarlo—when my words failed, hers did not.

We have much gratitude to the characters in this book:

Abet De Jeter, a troll by Bill Costanza. He is a water pipe fitter for the Riverside Water Company in California.

Anya, a fairy by Samantha Paitakis. She lives in New York and is a mother of four and an Interfaith Minister.

Gillie La Fleur, a fairy by Jayne Dion. She is an artist and designer living in California.

Norian, a wizard who remains anonymous. He lives on an island shaped like a fish.

Zankie Zanna, a fairy by Susann Gude. She lives in New York and is a photographer.

Rosy, Sweet Tea, and **Mrs. Nettle**—characters by Barbara Costanza.

Baby Fairy, a fairy who lives in the Fairy Forest.

REFACE

I am Barbara Costanza, author and creator of *The Fairy Forest*, which was inspired by my close friend Susann Gude who is a professor at SUNY Farmingdale, Visual Communications Department.

Susann had a vision and physically helped me in the woods on my property. Together, we cleared miles of pathways that we called the Fairy Woods. She also kept me motivated throughout the years with her photography and enthusiasm for the love of nature and its spirits. She inspired me to follow my dream and continue to be creative through difficult times.

My daughter, Melissa, is the main character and illustrator of the book. She allowed me to take her personal experience and incorporate it into this true-to-life story. She is one of my three best creations and life's special gift. There are not enough words to express my gratitude for her hard work and her patience while completing the vision I had for this story.

I want to acknowledge my husband and sons for giving me love and encouragement to write this book, for which I am forever grateful.

In the fairy woods with family and friends, we continue to have enchanted parties and scavenger hunts. Adults and children make fairy houses along the pathways. This is a magical place for walks and meditations. I hope to maintain and preserve our woods so the nature's elements can spark the imaginations of future generations. I also thank my spirit guides with all my heart.

In memory of my son

Cliff Anthony Costanza

His playfulness and pure love lives on in our hearts forever..

The Fairy Forest

In a small town called Patchogue, there is a secluded piece of wooded land preserved for fairies to live in.

These particular woods are located on Long Island, a fish-shaped island off the east coast of North America. This small area of woods is centered at the belly of the fish.

A freshwater creek winds through the woods and wetlands out to a saltwater bay. During the day, you can see mud turtles, muskrats, blue herons, ducks, swans, geese, and on occasion, wild turkeys. At night, the land is roamed by raccoons, opossums, deer, and of course, the neighborhood cats. They all come out to watch the moonlit woods come alive with movement.

The Patchogue Indians were the first people to live in these woods. Indians have spirit guides, which are usually in the form of the animals that are living in the woods with us today.

Our Fairy Forest is two acres with a mile of winding pathways for walking—about 5,300 footsteps. If you look carefully, you will find fairy houses of all sizes nestled in the shrubs and trees. The air is scented with pine trees laced with the salty, moist breeze from the bay. Mother Nature has given us a special place to create and glimpse magic while allowing our imagination to run free.

We invited our friends to be part of an adventure. They have created their own special characters to join our fairy community here in Patchogue. We bring our fictional creatures to life in this book through illustrations and photography on location.

As you read our stories and view the pictures, we want to take you out of the real world for a little while to enjoy the fairy life.

We hope this book inspires you to see the beauty of nature's details and the beauty inside the minds of our fellow beings.

May your mind be open and your heart stay warm.

Thirty Some Years Ago

Some might say I was unusual; I really didn't see why. I simply didn't like to watch cartoons, play with dolls, wear dresses, or eat kid food. Instead I preferred to play outside in the woods, drink anything but soda, and I favored raw, chopped clams and sautéed liver. This was around the age of three.

My grandparents knew right away I was different. They never did mind watching me in the evening when my parents went out because at 6:00 p.m., I would put myself to bed in a dark room with the door closed—if I could stay awake that late.

When I was four years old, I liked to have a bath before going to bed. What reasonable four-year-old didn't?

At five years, I had a focused interest in animals and insects. I insisted on knowing how their babies were born, so my mother delicately explained it to me by drawing pictures of animals giving birth. This inspired in me a love of drawing, and I was quite good at it. With a nature book in one hand and paper and pencil in the other, I walked around the yard, drawing pictures of bugs and leaves.

Living in a small town in the country was perfect for me. My parents built a home in a private, wooded area that is not populated with a lot of other homes. There is a stream that flows through the middle of the property, and my father built a wooden bridge across it. In the middle is a little island furnished with a cement bench, which I fittingly named Bench Island. The stream was my favorite place to go and draw the leaves that floated on top of the water.

My mother said I was a happy little girl, singing and playing outside by myself for hours. She often worried that I did not have enough friends to play with, but I did not find that to be a problem. Why would I? I was never alone and never felt lonely.

After me came two younger brothers. We all grew up in the house we were born in. Two younger girls, family friends, grew up with us practically in the same house. All five of us agreed that our home and family life could not have been better.

*G*rowing Pains

I did not particularly care to go to school, so I was sick all the time. My mother worried and frequently brought me to the doctor. I loved our pediatrician. He asked my mother how I did in school, and the answer was that I was a well-rounded student with good grades. With a chuckle, he told my mother it wasn't necessary that I go to school when I did not feel well. He offered to write a letter to the school saying as much. He is the reason I decided to become a doctor. A good doctor knows just what it takes to heal someone.

So, needless to say, I only attended school three-quarters of the time. I graduated in the top percentile and was president of my class. My inspiring quote under my senior picture was "to attend a full week of school in college."

Life—as we all know—changes, and the study of holistic healing in graduate school kept my head in the books. In between all the schooling, I got married and gave birth to our child. The picture looked perfect, but the human experience was exhausting me. My job was to help patients heal: real people with real problems. My family's needs had to be met. My animal's needs had to be met. Like most adults, we tend to forget what our own needs are, and they go neglected.

On top of all life's frustrations, tragedy hit our family. My younger brother died. Many families experience loss, and they are the ones who know what real life changes are. We were fortunate enough to have the love and support of friends and family to help us cope with the tremendous loss.

Years have passed, and my heart is still broken. Life has not quite felt the same. I have tried many ways to get my warm heart back, but I still have not completely found it. Not until recently, anyway.

One day, when I was walking through the woods, I received an unexpected enlightenment. This true-to-life journey has opened up a new dimension for me.

Anyone in need of warming their heart is welcome to follow me on these emerald paths home. So sit in a comfortable chair and get a hot cup of tea and something sweet to eat. Let the room be quiet and travel into the woods with me. Leave your real world behind and, maybe, you can bring some of the magic back with you when you decide to return.

The Day It Began

My parents are away again. They are away more than they are home. They assume it's easy for me to find the time to check on their house, water their plants, and feed their cat—the cat that makes my family's eyes water and their noses run. I wish I could like this cat. It is so hot for June. The humidity has already saturated the air. I hate to have sticky hands.

Where is the cat?

Now I have to run around the yard looking for it.

What is that?

There stands a rusty gate to enter into the woods.

Who has the time or money to put up an eight-foot gate to decorate woods that no one goes into anymore?

I see there is nothing but overgrown paths that don't go anywhere but to more woods.

Oh, look at this—all the paths have been cleared. Only my mother would work all winter, making paths through the woods.

Who does that?

Then when it's the season for walking and the woods are all green, she leaves. She'd better come back soon because the poison ivy is in full bloom.

I shall take a quick walk through here in case the cat has gone this way.

I just pray I don't get a rash.

"Here, Kitty, Kitty!"

I don't remember there being so many bugs this time of the year; it is so annoying just being in here.

Ouch! What the heck, have I really just been stung by a bee? You have got to be kidding. *That really hurts! Run! Don't walk. Run, run.* I have just run out of my shoe. *Keep going. There are more bees chasing me. I can hear the buzzing sound.*

Oh great, my other shoe has gotten caught on a raised tree root. I am actually going down. Thirty years old is too old to fall, and it feels like slow motion. I'm already thinking about what part of my body will hurt the most, and I haven't even hit the ground yet.

Nice. Now I'm lying on my stomach with dirt in my mouth and leaves on my clothes, and the bee sting is killing me. If I were not alone, this would be funny. As it is, I don't find it amusing at all. I think I'll just lie here for a moment and catch my breath. Wow, the path looks different from this angle. I never noticed how green and soft the moss is. What is that crawling out of the bush? Please, not another bee. But that's not a buzzing sound I am hearing; it's more like a whisper.

Whoa, that is the biggest butterfly I have ever seen. Am I hearing sounds coming from a bug? Is it possible that I hit my head when I fell? I actually hear a voice saying to rub the bee sting with moss. I'm already lying on it, so I really have nothing to lose. I'll just move my leg across the moss . . . Hmm, that seems to work. No more pain.

Who said that? Did a butterfly just speak?

"I am not a butterfly. I am a fairy, and my name is Rosy."

A small, winged woman alights on the path.

After the bee episode, I fight an urge to swat it.

She says, "You are seeing me because I have decided to allow you to see me. I have been listening to your thoughts the entire time you have been in these woods, and I almost didn't recognize you—not because you have grown up, but because your mind has not grown at all."

I grab the notepad and pencil that I always have with me and begin to sketch this tiny figment of my imagination before I come to my senses. Instead of disappearing, like I expected she would, she poses for me.

As I start to open my mouth to speak, she warns me, "If you do not want me to go away, you cannot ask me any questions quite yet. It is my pleasure to be here for you, that is why we fairies exist at all. You have lost your spirit, and I will help you find it. Let's begin our walk from the gate where you first entered, and I will show you all the things you have missed." As we walk, Rosy tells me the story of how she came to live here in our woods.

Rosy

"Centuries ago, I was born in a rose garden in California. Roses, redwood, linden, dogwood, and flowering plum trees surround my birthplace. I lived harmoniously with the nature into which I was born. Fairies live very long lives, hundreds of years. Time does not exist to us. We live only in the moment, and each moment to its fullest.

"One morning, as I was sleeping in my rosebud, a loud, thumping noise woke me. It was the sound of footsteps on the ground that shook me out of my deep sleep. 'The grape pickers are here,' I shouted for all to hear.

"You see, years earlier, the farmers turned the land into vineyards to grow grapes. They make a bottled drink called champagne out of these grapes. This drink is a wonderful elixir to celebrate life. Eventually, the farmers opened the vineyards for people to tour, and every day brought the dangers of big, flat man shoes and spiked lady heels. It was no longer a safe place for us tiny fairies to dwell.

"'Oh, Rosy,' I said to myself, 'what should I do for my fairy family, who stand the risk of accidental death at the feet of humans?'

"So I made the decision to fly away in search of a safe, secluded place for us to live. I wrapped some goods in a grape leaf in preparation for a long flight and traveled east across the vast land of North America.

"I saw many different farms along the way, one more beautiful than the next. I flew and flew until I reached the other side of the country, eventually running out of land. My wings became very salty and damp from the ocean air, and it was time for me to stop and dry out.

"Slowly I made my descent on the island in New York that was shaped like a fish. It was quite different from my homeland. I spotted the patch of woods that was to be my new home and flew down to a small gathering of trees. Nestled on a pile of fallen tree branches was a house with a little working door just right for a fairy my size. It was embellished with blue and white beach glass. Inside I found a soft feather bed, so I settled in for a long, needed rest.

"Soon it was morning, and I was eager to explore this charming little place. As I flew through the woods, I discovered more tiny crafted homes, each with their own small door. One was more charming than the next. I had never seen a place more ideal for fairy living.

"Just then I heard a friendly sound. 'Hello,' chirruped a purple martin bird sitting high in a white pine tree. Purple martin birds have a leader that flies alone to seek out a safe home to bring their family to. A thought bubble popped out of my ear: *what a wonderful idea.*

"I asked the purple martin bird if he believed this was a safe place for fairies to live in. 'Yes,' he replied, truly believing it to be so.

"I then asked the bird if he would be so kind as to fly back west and tell my dear fairies to come here to make their home. And if he would be so kind, to spread the word throughout all fairy communities about the fish-shaped island where fairies are welcome to live.

"The bird was more than happy to do so, and I gave him a bag of freshly picked sunflower seeds to take along with him on his westward travels.

"The purple martin bird did his job well. He collected my family and told other fairies of the woods on the fish-shaped island. Joy filled the air as my family arrived, and newcomers were flying in daily. I did not know where to begin! With my wings fluttering as fast as a hummingbird's, I began preparing food, drinks, and bedding for the first arrivals.

"'Oh, Rosy, much to do, much to do,' I giggled with excitement. When I get too many ideas in my head, little bubbles start to come out of my ears—each one with a thought in it. I had to slow down. I didn't want to lose another thought.

"With a stick and dried grass, I made a broom and swept each home clean. I gathered wild berries and added some honey from a beehive and mixed it together for a delicious drink. I then picked tan mushrooms and squeezed milk from dandelion stems for a hearty, nourishing soup. With nuts and seeds, I made a crust for some gooseberry tarts.

"While impatiently awaiting the arrival of new fairies, I formed the beeswax into candles. When they are lit, they give off a warm golden glow. I placed moss in tree holes, which worked fine as soft beds for weary midnight travelers to sleep on.

"As the days passed, more fairies flew in—some on the wings of butterflies, some dropped off half asleep in the wee hours of the night by little brown bats. An old couple with a lantern in hand hopped in on the back of a large lumpy toad."

Fairy Community

"They all came in excited and exhausted, managing only short, friendly greetings to one another. The fairies were eagerly busy selecting their homes, and some even brought materials to build their own. The dear purple martin was now finished with his task and had returned to his own feathered nest high in the tree.

"So you see, the woods are now filled with fairies, my dear. All gifted with magical powers. They are all here for you. If you are willing to set your mind free and forget all you know, you will have your spirit back and find, once again, your heart's warmth."

I was so mesmerized by Rosy's story that I did not notice that she had led me back to the gate. The little fairy was gone, and I was walking absentmindedly toward my parents' house.

I don't remember much after that point, but I do remember going to feed the cat. He purred at me knowingly, as though he was well aware of everything that had just happened in the woods. His fur felt warm and soft under my hand.

I went home in a daze, not quite sure of what I had experienced. That night, I took a relaxing hot bath and went to bed early. It had been a long time since I had done that, and it felt great.

Tomorrow, I will make sense of it all.

ay 2

The next morning, I woke up early with more energy than usual. I grabbed my slacks to take to the dry cleaners, and as I emptied the pockets, out dropped a page from my sketchbook. It was lying on the floor with a picture of a girl looking up at me.

I made a cup of coffee, sat down, and stared at the picture. Suddenly, the face became familiar, and I remembered Rosy, the fairy I met in the woods.

Did this really happen to me, or was the stress that I have been under causing me to see things that were not really there?

It took a moment for me to decide that it really didn't matter because the thought of it made me feel good.

$\mathcal{T}$ransformation

It is still the morning hours when I get to my parents' home to feed the cat. I feel much differently about this chore today. I am almost looking forward to going there to see why it makes me feel so good. The woods are more inviting, and I know that when I walk through the gate, I am leaving my worries behind. I feel childlike, excited to see the early morning fog lift from the woods. I am searching through a gray mist to find the purple martin bird that Rosy had spoken about when suddenly I notice that my clothes are, well, transforming.

My hair is becoming a fall of purple feathers, and my black dress is now a matching feathered sheath. I have a strong sensation of taking flight. I begin to soar through the trees as though I am seeing them for the first time.

It is welcoming and warm on the sun-dappled paths of the woods. I am surrounded by a sense of safety and love, yet I am alone. I know that Rosy is here somewhere, watching me, but I do not see her.

Now I notice that my mother and her friends have made fairy houses and placed them throughout the woods along the paths. Is this what they were doing all winter long in the woods?

Upon closer inspection, I notice that the houses are all filled with handmade beds and furnishings, making them appear to be more like homes for tiny people. Is it possible that fairies really do exist?

Where is that sweet aroma coming from? It has the familiar smell of the apple pies I loved as a child. The scent immediately floods me with the comforting memories of eating fresh homemade pies right from the oven. While I try to follow the scent, I glimpse some movement in the tree. I hope it is the bird I am looking for.

No, it is not the shape of a bird but what appears to be a boy with a small crooked wing attached to his back. He is running and holding out his hand, in which he carries a steaming-hot apple pie. He slows down for a moment as I grab for my pencil. He grins and pauses just long enough for me to sketch him, and then he scampers off in a rush, leaving a powdery dust of cinnamon.

Rosy suddenly appears, hovering over a prickly thorn bush. As she licks sugar off her lips, she calls out, "Come fly with me, and I will tell you about Sweet Tea."

Sweet Tea

"Sweet Tea arrived in the middle of the day. Jumping off the tail of the purple martin bird, he claimed his home before anyone noticed he was even here. He chose a large hollowed log. Inside he placed a teacup fitted with a soft, squishy teabag. The teacup bed has an extravagant canopy made from a brightly colored feather duster—it was quite a find.

"Don't let this little fairy fool you. He can be a she, although fairies rarely change genders. He is a secret agent of the culinary arts and a master of disguise, you see.

"One time he was an old lady and got invited to a high tea. While the other ladies were chatting, he stole an eight-hundred-year-old recipe. I do believe it was the pumpkin, butternut, golden dumpling stew to be exact. The stew was a big hit served at his half-moon dinner party held a week later.

"His signature dish—from somebody else's secret family recipe—is magnolia bark, split bean crumble buns sprinkled with silky cocoa powder. It's very good for fairies' night vision.

"Another time, he turned himself into a chunk of cheddar cheese. He thought the visiting pig named Le Chard would put him in his basket of truffles and carry him to where the wild mushrooms grow.

"Instead, he was grabbed by a muddy swamp rat that ran for a mile before realizing he was inedible and dropped the cheesy boy in the reeds. Still, the other fairies have not caught on to his tricks—though I think his indiscretions would be forgiven, for his food fills bellies and feeds souls. He is a fine cook and not a bad spy. As long as he stays undercover, he may be just fine.

"When all fairies gather, Sweet Tea is first to know. He cooks up a savory storm and shares his fine provisions with all. From soups and stews, pies, cakes, and bread, he makes enough so all are fed."

As Rosy finishes telling me about him, I spot the hollowed-out log not far from where I stand. I kneel down to peek inside, and it is filled with antiquities. His teacup bed is China's finest.

I want to fly to each unique house and visit every fairy dwelling, but Rosy says, "Enough for one day. You must return to your own home now."

So we fly together through the gates, and I drop to the ground. Unexpectedly, the weight of the world quickly returns to my entire body. Ouch!

ay 3

I wake up this morning with a jolt of concern. It is surely the next day, and I am checking to see if I am losing my mind. My heart starts to pound as I reach for my sketchbook. I'm not sure if I want to see a drawing or not.

Slowly, I open the page. I can see the beginnings of pencil markings. There it is, a picture of a small boy sporting a crooked wing tied together with foxtail hairs.

He is grinning at me as if he knew it would be a shocking surprise.

It is!

$\mathscr{B}$aby Fairies

Now I can't wait to get to my parents' house to feed the cat.

When I arrive, I run through the gates, and a strong wind pushes behind me. I run as fast as I can along with the breeze.

The heady fragrance of wild roses fills the air and lifts my spirits even higher today.

I want to see, touch, and talk to all the fairies; where can I find them?

I can't stop, not even to catch my breath.

Just then, out of the corner of my eye, a baby fairy flies by. I charge after it, hoping to grab it.

As I dash along the paths, my clothes become transparent.

I am moving so fast I hardly notice that I am now barefoot and running in a gown the color of air. It feels light and refreshing, like the exhalation of a baby's breath.

$\mathcal{L}$ook but Don't Touch

The white sparkling shine from my dress is so bright, it causes me to lose sight of the baby. I stop near a tree so I can lean on it to catch my breath and brush off my feet. Looking down at the tree stump, I see a baby fairy curled up sound asleep. I pick it up carefully and hold it in the palm of my hand. I can't resist gently placing my lips on it to give it a kiss.

Abruptly, a loud shout rings out, scolding me, "Put that wee one down! You might crimp its wings." Rosy pounces on my big toe.

Ever so gently, I place the spotted fairy back while it remains deep in sleep, exactly how I found it.

As Rosy tries to distract me from the baby, a bubble floats up to my nose and pops. "I have an idea," she says. "Let's go down by the stream, and I will tell you about Mrs. Nettle."

I follow Rosy down to the narrow wooden bridge that crosses the stream. I listen to the familiar sound of the babbling water that flows underneath it. I hear what sounds like voices echoing in a tin can and notice a metal pot with a door cut into its side. A sign hangs from its lid, awaiting a closer look.

Rosy sits me along the side of the stream and tells me about the fairy named Nettle.

Mrs. Nettle

"Mrs. Nettle once lived in the stream with many beautiful nymphs of various colors borrowed from a rainbow. One rainy day, an ugly, grumpy troll named Nettle saw her cross over the bridge. Typically, a troll will give anyone a hard time when trying to cross a bridge. Trolls only get up on one side of the bed, and it's never the right one. When he saw this nymph, however, with her radiant skin and silky long hair, he fell in love with her instantly.

"He asked her to marry him. She gave it a quick thought and said yes. She is kindhearted and can only see the beauty in other creatures. Through her eyes, Nettle is a handsome, thoughtful troll.

"They lived very happily together for years until one night, a thick fog rolled in. By morning, the fog had lifted, and her husband was gone.

"Mrs. Nettle was sad and lonely. She would sit and stare into the stream all day long, hoping her husband would reappear. All she ever saw were the toads that sat on the lily pads beside her.

"One day, just as the morning sun was rising, she was looking at her reflection in the stream through teary eyes and saw something shining on top of the water. There it was, a large silver pot floating down the stream under the troll bridge. She climbed inside and claimed it as her home. The muskrats helped her lift it onto the mossy bank. She called it her Kettle to honor her love for Nettle. So was the start of the unique, metal home, where she opened her door to all who felt alone.

"The pot is a place to go for a cup of brew or bittersweet nectar. It is a place to go to talk to one another and vent about fairy woes. Every creature and fairy has a story to tell. "She hung out a sign, calling her pot the Mettle Kettle for all the fairies to see, to encourage strength and fortitude in the creatures that needed it the most. So this is the place to go to get to know one another."

The Kettle that serves as a meeting place for the fairies to gather and make acquaintances is so intriguing. I insist that Rosy tell me more. I ask her if trolls do actually live here in our woods.

Rosy clears her throat and giggles. "Well, my dear, it starts with the first day you arrived in the woods. The tree root you tripped on was not quite there by accident. It was lifted off the ground intentionally by a troll named Abet. Abet lives near the forest in an underground home made of roots close to the water, so he tends to be a bit cranky and damp.

"When I first met him, I said hello, and this was his reply."

Abet De Jeter

"'Hi, how are you doing today? I'm Abet, and yes, I am a troll. First off, I just want to set the record straight: not all trolls are disgruntled. The discrimination needs to stop, thank you.

"'My full name is Abet De Jeter. My parents thought it would be clever to name me after these running waters. I was born and raised right here at Abet's Creek. Okay, so not all trolls are clever either. What the fairies fail to realize is that trees live in need of water to survive. Trees get water from their root system. That is where I come in, me being a pipe-root fitter. I am constantly fixing root leaks caused by the overgrowing fairy population.

"'Look, fairies can be destructive from time to time. Sometimes they behave like common squirrels, flushing pine needles, acorn lids, pebbles, and all kinds of forest coverings down the root system daily. It breaks roots,'" said Rosy, imitating Abet's scowl. "'They just don't listen!

"'Now we have a fancy fairy from Paris living here, and she's just as clumsy as a mole in daylight. She's only been here a week, and somehow she's managed to get stuck in a skunk leaf, a smelly ordeal, and crash-landed into an oak seedling! That poor little tree is a mess—it'll take months to fix. *But Miss La Fleur is a looker, so I cut her a break. I wonder how she feels about trolls . . .*

"'Anyway, it is up to me to keep the trees happy, to keep the forest happy, and to keep the fairies happy. It can be demanding at times. So the next time you come across a grumpy troll under a tree or bridge, remember he's probably just working on fixing something. So throw him a bone and wish him adieu!'"

Rosy laughs. "He then rushed off to help Gillie La Fleur with her skirt, which she somehow managed to get snagged in the sticky weeds."

Rosy continues telling me about Gillie. Speaking in her best French accent, she recounts the story of the clumsy fairy.

Gillie La Fleur

"Feeling falsely accused of mischievous deeds, Gillie rummaged through her personal belongings, fretting about what to take with her on the long journey to a new colony of fairies on the island shaped like a fish. Would she ever return to her native land of France again?

"Gillie La Fleur actually lived in a French boutique in New York City, just minutes from Long Island. But having never left the store, she thought she was a natural-born Parisian.

"The honeybees had overheard the purple martin bird talk about the safe new woods. Gillie received the news as the bees gossiped while they bounced about, collecting their pollen from the flower boxes. She had to hurry if she was going to catch the next swarm of bees heading to the woods before the queen bee changed her mind on where to build her hive. Gillie was well aware of the dangers an unescorted fairy could encounter while traveling so far. She had to take the ladybugs along with her. What was a refined Parisian fairy to do without her ladybugs-in-waiting? She packed her full ruffled skirts and lace parasols but had to leave her lavish cottage furnishings behind. She instructed the slugs to keep them well polished until she sent word to have her heirlooms brought to her across the seas.

"Gillie believed she used proper manners and diction when engaging in conversation and that she was always on time to cotillions or tea. Always impeccably dressed, she thought of herself as elegant and graceful, whether in a garden or ballroom setting. Unfortunately, she wears so many layers of skirt petals that she cannot see where her feet are going. She is constantly knocking over glassware, tables, and toadstools, sending unsuspecting fairies flying into the air. Luckily, there are resourceful fairies to keep up with the damages she leaves behind."

Rosy stands up and tugs on my hair. It is time for me to leave; the sun is nearly setting. As I walk back to the gate, my gown begins its transformation back to the clothes I had worn earlier. The whole time, I am thinking how fancy it will be to buy a full ruffled skirt. I will wear it for dancing, to spin and twirl, so shopping I will go.

Open-Minded

My world is changing so quickly. I have found a place where fairies actually do exist.

Each morning I wake to view the sketches I drew the day before. When I return to the woods, I will try to find all their homes nestled in the trees and shrubs. I have become accepted by these magical creatures that live to help us humans with all our difficulties. They come in the day or night—whenever they are needed the most.

Tonight I lie in bed, drifting off to sleep, snuggling under my own feathered quilt with a vision of tranquil waters and fairies that fly.

$\mathcal{D}$ay 4

I leave my house at daybreak before my family awakens. I arrive at my parents' house and quickly feed the cat, anxious to see what is in store for me today.

I enter the woods very quietly, observing each branch as I walk in. The early morning sun is peeking through the leaves; the woods are peaceful and serene.

I whisper for Rosy, and all I hear is a low, deep breathing. There is a slim house with a pointed roof stuck on the side of a tree. The figure of a robed man is standing on the edge of the cedar limb next to it. His arms are extended in a very odd position.

"Who are you?" I yell up to him.

When he does not answer, I yell louder.

He answers me now in a long drawn-out exhale, "Norian."

Rosy, out of breath, whispers in my ear, "Do not disrupt the wizard's concentration. He is doing the ancient exercise, Qigong."

Rosy and I watch this bearded man perform a breathing ritual.

After catching her own breath, Rosy tells me about Norian.

orian

"The sun was about to rise when I first met Norian," Rosy says, telling her story. "I heard deep belly laughter and followed the sound. High upon the tree branch he stood, breathing in, his arms rounded, knees slightly bent, gazing out at the horizon. Norian was performing his morning practice. The air was still, crisp, and lightly scented with cedar. As the sun gracefully rose, his breathing was slow and full, his movements precise. He was focused on the energy all around him. Qi energy is abundant in the air, water, and food. It is the same energy that gives us life. If we can take the time to be still and cultivate it, amazing feats are possible.

"As Norian finished his routine, a feeling of gratitude filled his being, and he walked mindfully toward a basin. Reaching in with cupped hands, he rinsed his face. As the water settled, he took a long, hard look at his reflection staring back at him. His bright smile shone with the light of the sun. His blue-green eyes glistened like the surface of the ocean and were filled with years of wisdom. While wringing out his beard, Norian let out a sigh of satisfaction.

"He headed toward the small garden a few yards from his humble home to gather some mint for his morning tea. Once inside, he strategically placed another log on the fire as the steaming vat began to hum. He poured his tea and invited me in to join him in front of the fire.

"Norian has lived by himself for many years in the mountains. His favorite snack is goji berries and pure cocoa. He loves how the flavors complement each other and give him nourishment. He always carries some in a pouch when he takes his daily hikes. Sweet Tea disguised himself as a praying mantis and perched alongside Norian. He knew Norian would feed him from his pouch. But not knowing the power in his special mixture, Sweet Tea was charged with overflowing energy for weeks."

Rosy pauses to giggle.

"Norian came to the island to experience life closer to the water level, away from the high mountains he was used to. He is comfortable sitting high in the trees, where he can look down to watch over all of us. On cool days, he can be spotted relaxing in abandoned squirrel nests while enjoying his pipe and taking in the view. Little does he know that I watch him too," says Rosy. Again she lets out a giggle, and a bubble pops out of her ear.

I wonder what idea she is thinking of next.

Resting by the Indian Pipes

Rosy and I find a small place to rest. I start taking in deep breaths of air and feeling so relaxed.

"Rosy, the fairies are all so different from one another. Do they all show themselves to people as they have to me?" I ask.

"Only if their hearts are ready to see them." She sighs.

It is a peaceful moment sitting in the woods, watching butterflies flutter by. As I gaze down at the stream through the branches, I see a slender young lady walking a younger little girl to the water. I nudge Rosy because I did not recognize her to be Mrs. Nettle.

In a very sweet voice, Rosy tells me she is Anya, the baby-fairy caretaker.

Rosy lies down on a twig bed near a patch of Indian pipes. She tells me the story of Anya as if she were in a daydreaming state of mind.

Rosy begins to explain, "It was a chilly evening when she flew in escorted by two white doves. Upon her arrival, the air temperature rose eleven degrees to warm us up that night."

Anya

"Anya lived on a small island in the middle of the Great Lakes. It is called the Isle of Graciousness. Fairies from the isle have an innate consciousness to be gracious. They are always kind and compassionate in every way.

"Their surroundings are of pure beauty, and each living being on the isle emits an individual sound that only fairies can hear. Each of the fairies has their own sound that creates a soothing melody. Human children are able to hear it in their deepest sleep.

"Anya followed the purple martin in the sky, leaving trails of swirling energy with sparkling colors human eyes can only see in their dreams. Anya's purpose is to help all living things. She inspires human children to remember their own special sound inside them. Therefore, they always know they are a part of the song of creation.

"As the baby fairy caretaker, she lulls them to sleep. Her songs remind her of the many animals on the isle she left behind, the shashabees, shmoogmoogies, and even her beloved pixifoos, who all await patiently for her return.

"Anya's love for islands has brought her here. She walks the little ones to the water's edge and shares her knowledge with them. So when she leaves the little fairies are empowered to do the same, to carry on the nurturing musical rhythm the fairy caretakers possess."

Rosy expresses her own gratitude for having this lovely fairy here in the woods to care for the teensy ones as the fairy population continues to grow.

I think that Anya lulls all the fairies to sleep with her sound; I wonder if Rosy is aware of that too.

New Arrivals

It is so peaceful. Rosy and I start to doze off in the shadow of a tree when a bright light flashes all around us. We see what looks like lightning strikes hitting the ground; through my squinted vision, I see a fairy pounce down.

"That's Zankie Zanna!" Rosy exclaims, rubbing her eyes. "She can't just watch us quietly. She always needs to capture our attention."

"Keep your eyes closed, and she will move on quickly." Rosy yawns.

I tighten my eyelids as hard as I can, and sure enough, off she flies down the path.

My curiosity makes me impatient; with blurry vision, I plead to Rosy to tell me more.

Rosy can't resist telling me another story, so with my eyes closed and ears open, I listen intently.

Zankie Zanna

"Zankie arrived in the community as fast as a flash, her brilliant colors sparking off her. Her landing was so brightly lit, the fairies had to close their eyes. As her feet touched the ground, she yelled, 'Let us return to loving all creatures, humans, animals, and nature spirits!' Her introduction was so thunderously enthusiastic that fairies had to cover their ears as well.

"Dressed in shimmering colors and decorated with colored crystals, she is a rather attractive fairy. But if you look closely at the middle of her forehead, you will notice that something is amiss. She has a third eye right between the expected two. With this extra eye, she can capture and record everything around her. Zankie knows the past is present, and the present will pass.

"Zankie has recorded mystical places from all over the world—and many out of this world too. On special occasions, she will show these other worlds to the ones that believe in taking care of the one on which they live.

"Her talent can be entertaining when she shows the community their own memories in a spectrum of color. Her little assistant named Bunny is as quick as one too. Bunny cleans off her lens for a clearer view.

"Zankie Zanna records the fairies dancing in the fairy circle. She spins and spins to follow along, and at times, she gets quite dizzy. Many fairies are in awe of her ability and want to be captured in her recordings, but there are others who worry that their magic may be overexposed and revealed to the world. There are wild tales about Zankie Zanna. Sometimes you can hear them being told.

"She lives in an old movie projector from the year 1920. It has a radiant silver-and-teal rooftop, so when it rains, she stays warm and dry. Zankie calls her home the Reel Place. It is nestled on the ground floor of the woods, visible for all to see.

"She makes sure that not an event gets missed. With her third eye, she records and stores it all for us to recall. If memory fails us, Zankie comes to our aid and reminds us of the joyful times we've forgotten. From trolls to pixies to human beings, she shines her light on all."

Reflections

I leave the woods at the end of the day filled with an inner peace from the fairies that I met. I think of the forgotten childhood memories and wonderful images shown to me by Zankie Zanna. Mrs. Nettle encourages me to open my doors and welcome others in. The ancient wisdom of Norian to live simply, breathe deeply, and allow myself to laugh. Anya taught me to listen to the vibrations of unconditional love. I learn to understand a grumpy troll, to dress up and dance like Gillie La Fleur. Sweet Tea taught me not to be afraid of who I am and to appreciate others for who they are.

I reflect on the morals of Rosy's teachings too. If we care for ourselves as well as we do for others, we can find perfect balance here on earth.

The future is now looking much brighter for me.

ay 5

I wake up this morning feeling in balance with my life and the world around me until I realize that my adventures with the fairies will soon come to an end. My mood slowly gives way to sadness. A sudden sense of fear makes me impulsively rush to my parents' house. I charge through the gate, expecting it all to be gone.

Once again, to my surprise, it is anything but. Flashes of sparks fly from every direction. The woods are alive with sound and movement. The wind blows, the leaves rattle, and the trees creak. Mice squeak, toads croak, crickets chirp, and birds sing. It is the most beautiful music I have ever heard. A celebration of fairies comes parading through the woods.

Norian and Zankie frolic with laughter on the mossy knoll. Mrs. Nettles strolls down the path, arm in arm with Sweet Tea, cookies and cakes in hand. Anya guides the babies down the trail on the backs of tree snails. Gillie La Fleur does pirouettes along the path to the fairy ring with Abet De Jeter following behind, trying to hold and fix her broken parasol at the same time.

When they reach the middle of the fairy ring, they circle around, facing the center with anticipation. Rosy flies to my ear and tells me, "There is one more spirit for you to meet."

Just as she finishes her last word, a brilliant point of white light begins to glow above the circle. The fairies link hands as the light grows larger; barely discernable is a spirit of an indeterminate age. His warm brown eyes dance with mischief, and his perfectly formed mouth turns up at the corners. He laughs and thousands of sparks fill the deep green forest.

The light that surrounds him is pure love, and I immediately understand that my sibling's spirit will always be with me. The warmth of his light fills the coldest parts of my body, and I gasp at the rush of familiarity. And then he is gone.

The smiling fairies look up at me. One by one, they disappear in pops of white light. I am left exhilarated, healed in places that I thought would be wounded forever.

Rosy is the only fairy that remains. She looks at me, winks, and tells me it is time for me to return to my own family.

Exiting the Fairy Forest

Although I do not want to see the fairies go, I know that the memories in these woods will always be here for me to roam through.

"Will you stay with me, Rosy?"

"I have never been gone" is her last reply.

Just then, my parents' car comes rolling down the driveway, and the horn sounds. When I turn, Rosy disappears.

My parents get out of the car, and the cat runs over to greet them. My mother notices that I am standing by the gate, and she immediately knows that something has happened to change me. She puts her arm around me, and we walk to the house in silence.

Just before we go through the doorway, my mother turns to look back at the gate. She appears to be smiling at someone, and she nods with approval.

"It's nice to be home." She sighs. "Come in and sit down. I have so much to tell you about our adventures."

The door closes gently behind me, and the cat begins to purr.

Printed in the United States
By Bookmasters